I0764349

Sea Trials

A Stella Madison Caper

Lilly Maytree

LIGHTSMITH PUBLISHERS
Thorne Bay, Alaska

ISBN: 978-1-944798-26-0

Lightsmith Publishers
P.O. Box 19293
Thorne Bay, AK 99919

www.LightsmithPublishers.com

Cover photography by Steve and Becky Brown

Quantity sales ordering information:
Special discounts are available on quantity purchases by corporations, associations, and others. For details, contact the info@LightsmithPublishers.com

Sea Trials / LTB paperback edition

Published in the United States of America

To all those wonderful people who have stood by their friends during difficult times and been brave enough to step out into the unknown together.

"The longer I live, the more convincing proofs I see of this truth – that God governs in the affairs of men."

Benjamin Franklin

1

Stella Madison flinched when a cold splash of spray hit her face and she tightened her hold on the bouncing rail. The motorboat was loaded to full capacity, with Colonel Oliver P. Henry's large bulk ensconced precisely in the middle for better balance. She and her friend Millie (who had insisted on wearing a bright orange life preserver) were at the very front, practically hanging over the bow. Gerald and Lou were in the last seat behind the Colonel, while the Captain stood up in the stern with a casual grip on the tiller and the outboard turned up to full throttle. The Senator was riding like a king in a backpack-type apparatus attached to his mother.

"E-gads!" Gerald complained as they bounced off another ripple of chop and sped through the darkness. "I say – is it necessary to go all out?"

"It is if we want to get out of this bay before ten o'clock," answered Captain Stuart, whose gray hair was standing up all over like a wild man in the wind.

It was six thirty-seven in the morning. On a Sunday.

Just as Stella began to wonder what in the world she had let herself in for, Stuart cut the motor to half-power and they spent the next ten minutes weaving in and out around the dark shapes and shadows of other boats anchored across the bay. The sky was still black as night. While her hurried breakfast of donuts and coffee was beginning to churn with a mind of its own, a great ominous wall gradually emerged out of the darkness. The Captain turned the little craft smartly, and cut the motor. He tossed a line over a cleat as they drifted up against a floating wooden platform, and then jumped out to run forward and secure the bow.

"Here we are, mates!" he crowed. "Go

easy – one at a time, now – it's too early to have to fish anybody out of the water!"

Stella climbed out and stepped gingerly onto the rocking platform with a distinct sense of vertigo and nothing to hang on to. Just as she began to sink to her knees to keep from falling, she felt Captain Stuart's strong grasp under her arm and he propelled her forward to a dangling metal stairway. It stretched diagonally up against the wall – who cared where it went – as long as it took her away from here. She clutched the cold wet rail and began to climb. If she had tried to wait for the Colonel, she fully believed she would have thrown up.

There was a light on at the top and she recognized Millie's carpenter friend, Mason, as he reached out to help her step up and over onto the deck. At least she thought it was a deck. What it looked like was some narrow alleyway in the industrial section of the city, along with a row of metal doorways with round windows that disappeared into the feeble circle of light over the stairs.

"Top o'the morning, Stella!" Mason said with a contrived accent and obvious excitement for the occasion.

"Oh, Mase! You better help Lou – I don't know how she's going to cart that baby of hers all the way up here!"

"She's in better shape than any of us, old girl. But don't worry, she's used to it. We come out here every Fourth of July to watch the fireworks. Last time she was pregnant, so this time she'll think it's a breeze. Here comes Mil."

Millie handed over a large picnic basket, packed to the brim while she maneuvered out of her orange life preserver. "Hi, Mase – been up all night?"

"Well, it happens I have, and I could sure use a--"

"Come on, Stella!" Her friend beamed as if the excitement were infectious. "I'll show you the galley – you'll just love it!"

The Dreadnaught was a monstrous old schooner nearly eighty feet long that looked as if it had been around since the early days of sail. Over the years it had by turns been used to carry cargo, transport passengers, and had even done a stint in the fishing trade. Though it still sported an entire set of working canvas, it had once run on steam, but—somewhere down the line—been converted over to diesel. To Stella, it looked like some ancient but perpetual work in progress. But Millie was right about the galley.

It boasted a magnificent iron cook-stove that was plumbed for propane (but could also burn wood), a huge wooden table carved out of genuine Philippine mahogany, set between large comfortable settees that (even though faded and grease-stained) had once been covered in an expensive burgundy plush. Above it hung a fancy brass lantern that swung gently back and forth to the barely noticeable rocking of the sea beneath them. Plenty of counter space. Two deep stainless steel sinks that were every cook's dream…and the cupboards! Stella was sure such storage could never be found in a kitchen on land.

And, as if that weren't enough, there was a walk-in pantry the size of a small room just for laying in food supplies. According to Millie. At the moment, Stuart was using it as a paint locker.

"I'm going to take this cabin, here," Millie

dragged her – still gawking – through a shuttered wooden door with an adorable brass knob that was just to the left of the stove. “Cook’s quarters. What do you think?”

It was at that moment Stella was bitten with the same infectious excitement she had seen in all the others. Why it was another trip back in time! Like Casablanca and the Orient Express all rolled into one. An exotic little stateroom with mahogany woodwork all around; a bed off in one corner that sported (though faded and dusty) a palm-print spread; and a round brass porthole that opened right up over the sea. Stella could tell because she caught a waft of the moist salt air coming through.

“There’s even enough room to set up my favorite rocker.” Millie pointed to an area near the porthole, as she refastened her thick auburn hair back up into the clip the long strands had sprung loose from. “I can’t wait to get all my things in.”

“I had no idea!”

“Let’s go look at the Captain’s quarters.” With cheeks still flushed from the early morning boat ride, Millie propelled her reluctantly back through the galley and down some long interior companionway. "It's where you and the Colonel get to stay."

"What?" Stella felt her own color rising at the thought, and wondered how long it would take to get used to the fact she was Mrs. Oliver P. Henry, now. Married to the Colonel (retired), who had spent his career as a military historian.

"Stella, it's the perfect place for newlyweds. Just wait till you see this!"

"If that's the case, why don't you and Mason get the honor?"

"Are you kidding? I love him but we need our space. We'd be at each other's throats if we actually had to live together. Know what I mean?"

"Not really. But what about Stuart, then? He's the Captain, isn't he? Why doesn't he take the best apartment?"

"Stuart's something of an inventor. Always tinkering and making modifications on his engine. He wouldn't be happy anywhere but down in the engine room in the Chief Engineer's cabin. Been down there for years, and all this just stays empty. He's even got television down there!"

The companionway grew darker the farther they moved away from the light in the galley, but Millie seemed to know where she was going and kept plowing ahead with Stella still in tow. At the end of the narrow hallway, a few moments were devoted to pushing open a thick wooden door that obviously hadn't been moved for ages.

"It'll take some cleaning up, of course," Millie switched on a light attached to the nearest wall that sported a tattered red shade with tassels, right out of the era of speak-easies and bootleg liquor. "But did you ever see such extravagance?"

Extravagance wasn't the word for it.

The paneling was a rich mahogany, inlaid with various mermaids and sea creatures over each doorway and window. Half the back wall was a slanted bank of French windows, complete with tufted window seat beneath. Stella could just make out the outline of the sea from the faint glow of dawn that was beginning to spread over the sky. Beneath that was a gray plaid sofa with carved wooden curlicues arching over the back and arms, that ended in legs that were bolted to the floor. Part of the dark floor was covered over by a gaudy red and black Oriental rug that also seemed to be tacked down.

There was a huge desk off in one corner with a leather swivel chair behind – Oliver would like that, no doubt – the perfect place to sit and work by the hour without missing what the weather was behaving like outside, or hear what was happening up on the decks above. And for Stella, there were bookshelves everywhere. Only a few scattered and dusty volumes tipped over to occupy them now, but she could already foresee her own collection displayed in a comforting array all around, just waiting to be perused on dull evenings. The last thing she had expected on this venture was luxury. Things were definitely looking up.

Her eye traveled across to the wall opposite the desk, and there was the most –

"There you are!" Mason's voice boomed from the open doorway, where he stood with a half-finished chicken leg in hand. "Stuart wants everyone to--"

"Mason Jeferies!" Millie complained, " It's too early to be digging into the lunch!"

"But I'm half-starved, Mil. Been up working most of the night, and the only food ol' Stuart keeps around here are sardines and crackers, or boiled eggs. A man's got to have more than--"

"Oh, come on, then, and I'll fix you a ham sandwich." She headed back down the hall toward the galley.

"Stuart wants us all up on deck in about ten minutes, Stella," he said before turning to follow Millie. "So we can get started."

"All right," Stella answered. "I'll be along in a minute."

This because she needed another minute to finish exploring her new home, and maybe pinch herself once, or twice, to make certain this was all really happening. There was something "other worldly" about the place – no denying it – and the sudden feeling of "déjà vu" she experienced the moment she was left alone, proved it. How else could everything feel so familiar? Take that darling little wood-burning stove, for instance.

She knew exactly how it worked already. One simply lifted the small iron handle from its perch near the black pipe that went up through the ceiling, and used the hook end to lift one of the round burner covers that lead to the firebox below. Then one could regulate the amount of flame or coals necessary to –

She dropped the iron ring and jumped back as if it had burned her. And there it was, another one of those stabbing memories that came and went so fast one couldn't quite make it out. Along with the full-blown vision of a woman. But she had never seen such a woman! A beautiful young woman lifting one of the lids to that stove, with her dark hair all done up like one of the old-fashioned Gibson Girls. But she was wearing a man's clothes and there was a cigarette dangling from one corner of her mouth…

Impossible! It was all in her mind – it had to be – for there was no one else standing at this cold little stove that obviously hadn't been lit for years. "Oh, dear--" she murmured to herself, as she slowly backed away from it.

"Surely not this, again – not now!" No doubt it was the stress and strain of having to move, again, so soon. That's what it had to be.

"Are you all right, my dear?" How long had the Colonel been standing behind her? "Not feeling seasick, are you?"

2

"Not any more," Stella replied with a quick smile. "What do you think, Oliver? These are the Captain's quarters and everyone decided you and I should move in here."

"Magnificent desk!" He went over to try out the leather-upholstered chair and open and close a few of the drawers. "Comfortable, too. I have a feeling I could do my best work here, Stel."

"Oh, I know you can!" How distinguished he looked sitting there with that head of gray curls, his deep tan, and such a delightfully comfortable gaze. A lot more like a captain than that grizzly old Stuart. "And it will be even better by the time I get it all fixed up for us. Wait and see. I have to admit I was a little skeptical when we first came aboard but I'm thoroughly won over, now. I caught the fever from Millie."

"Sea fever?"

"Well, traveling fever, anyway." She took her purse off her shoulder and pulled a red bandana from one of its pockets to tie around her hair. She had a feeling the short white fluff that normally framed her face and tucked under neatly at the back, must be standing on end about as much as Captain Suart's was on that wild ride across the bay. "Don't know what kind of crew member I'll end up making but I'll certainly give it my best shot."

"As you do everything, my dear. It's one of the things I like best about you." He got to his feet. "Now, I suppose we should get back out on deck before Stuart starts bellowing orders."

Stella had not been put to so much physical exertion since the early days of her single life, when she was a substitute for high school P.E. Up with the sails, down with the sails, heave ho, and prepare to come about! Over and over again until she thought she was beginning to see double. What's more, these were enormous sails that took at least two of them to fully raise. Nobody was in shape.

Except maybe Stuart, who kept popping up unexpectedly in one place or another to bellow, "Harder! Put some back into it! We're trying to sail here – not set up tents! Blast it – Gerald – you're out of sync with everybody, again. Let's do it over!" And in the meanwhile, steering the boat, tending or shutting down the engine, and generally running circles around everybody.

When they broke for lunch at noon, everyone was so exhausted there were serious doubts about the whole endeavor. Only the baby seemed to be in his element, swinging contentedly between the starboard rail and a cabin corner, harnessed into some bouncing contraption called a "Johnny Jumper" that Mason had jury-rigged for him to play in. Millie's efforts at serving lunch amounted to little more than flopping open the top of the picnic basket and letting everyone fend for themselves. After that they were all granted a bit of "liberty" to regain their composure.

The Dreadnaught was anchored just far enough out in the channel to make the city and surrounding mountains look picture perfect nestled between a blue sky and slate green sea. Stella knew they were "at anchor" because they had dropped and hauled the thing back in again, at least four times during training maneuvers. She knew starboard was right and port was left, and forward and aft meant front and back respectively. Now all time seemed to be suspended in its tracks just to wait for them to pick things up again.

Everything felt incredibly peaceful.

What little wind there had been in the morning was almost completely gone and the sea was in a state of such flat calm inside the bay that she had to try very hard to feel even the slightest twinge of seasickness. After Lou settled the Senator down with an exhausted Gerald (who performed quite remarkably for someone living on disability) for a nap in one of the main deck cabins, she returned to where Stuart was tinkering with something mechanical back on the afterdeck.

"Can I fish for a while, Cap?" She set an icy can of root beer down on the deck beside him, and popped the top off an orange soda for herself.

"Didn't bring any bait this trip."

"How 'bout I use a chicken bone?"

"Suit yourself. You know where everything is."

Stella sipped at her cold tea and watched from the comfort of a faded blue deck chair pulled out into the sun. The Colonel was dozing in another deck chair beside her with his feet propped up on a nearby winch drum and his head leaned back against the smooth teak railing in front of the row of cabins. Millie had retired to her cook's quarters, and she had no idea where Mason had disappeared.

"I'm going to catch you a big yellow tail tuna for supper," Lou Edna announced.

"I'll wager five bucks you won't catch anything but mackerel, barracuda, or shark with that stuff," Stuart replied without looking up from his project. "Ain't any of which I like to eat."

"Orientals eat all those things," the young woman bantered.

"Yeah, and they eat bugs and rodents, too."

"Prejudiced, are you?"

"Not me. I was married to a Japanese gal once after the War. Doesn't mean I have to like eating junk food though."

"Junk food!" Lou Edna laughed and ignored the thin strap of her green tank top that slipped off her shoulder as she cast her line over the rail. "This generation junk food means a hamburger and fries."

"Now them I like."

Stella didn't quite know what to make of Lou Edna. The lies and taking advantage of Millie with rent and babysitting money had made her feel critical of the girl, at first. On the other hand, she was clearly attached to them all, as if Millie and Mason were surrogate parents and Gerald some favorite Uncle. The Colonel she seemed a bit wary of. Probably because he was indifferent to the ruses she used so freely on the others and made no effort to play along with her games. But for the most part she was polite with him.

Watching her easy banter with Stuart – Stella couldn't help wondering what the girl was really after. Because it was obvious this supple blonde-haired beauty that smelled all over like tanning oil today, was definitely after something. Stella had seen enough of her kind in the high schools she used to teach in to practically recognize them on sight.

Yes, Lou Edna was after something. The tears of last night had come and gone too quickly for such a hardened student of the rough life. Millie had also mentioned something about the girl having been raised in a long series of foster homes. But what really had Stella stumped was that it just didn't seem right how someone with the responsibility of a baby could so flippantly leave a decent paying job to trot off into the unknown where there might not be any job waiting at all. Did she think the "family" would simply take care of her and the Senator indefinitely? Stella could see how they all probably would, though, because that baby was about as cute as they came.

With a sudden squeal of delight that ended in a peal of musical laughter, Lou Edna began reeling in her line as fast as she could. It had been out there less than ten minutes. Just when Stella was thinking these waters must be teaming with fish, Lou tossed the empty pole down on the deck and proceeded to bounce up and down along the length of the rail as she waved at someone in the far off distance.

"Over here!" she cupped her hands to her mouth and yelled. "Woooo-hoo! Over here, Cole!"

Which brought the Colonel awake with a start, and the Captain to his feet to see who it was. Stella got up, too, arriving at the rail just in time to catch sight of an open speedboat that came smartly up alongside and cut the motor.

"Hey–" said a dark-haired young man with a beautiful smile who was sitting on the seat back instead of the cushion as he drove. "Looks like I found you."

"You sure did!" beamed Lou. "Got any ideas? This old man here's working my tail off. On a Sunday, too!"

"Want to drive out to one of the islands?"

"She's putting in for a position," Stuart answered for her, "and I haven't decided, yet."

"Oh, come on, Cap…" Lou Edna leaned against the older man and lowered her voice in a confidential whisper. "You know I've got everything down already, and I'm the strongest deckhand you've got so far. Right?"

"Well…"

"I need a little fun before I leave."

"What kind of fun?" Mason came up behind them and cast a glance over the rail. "Who the devil's that?"

"Cole Deforio." The young man gave a nod of his head then turned his brown eyes back to Lou. "You coming, or not?"

"Sure, but I have to wait until the Senator wakes up. Why don't you come aboard and meet everybody?"

"I'd be happy to watch him for you, Lou," Stella interjected quickly – the thought of taking a baby into that minuscule little boat! "If you'd like to go, that is. Seems a long trip to be starting out so late in a small open boat like that." Why, she had heard it was nearly six miles across open ocean even to get to the nearest island. After the bumpy adventure she had personally experienced this morning just crossing the calm harbor, the entire idea was appalling.

"Oh, would you, Stel? That would be great! He hasn't been feeling the best lately, anyway. I think he's got a bug, or something."

"No doubt."

"OK, change of plans – I'm coming down." Lou Edna reached for the black windbreaker she had tossed onto the deck earlier and fairly skipped toward the bow. "Pick me up under the anchor chain," she called over the noise of the motor as her young man started the engine, again. "And don't you dare let me fall in!"

Naturally, everyone followed. They lined up along the rail to watch her crawl up and over with an agility only the young possessed. As Cole expertly maneuvered his little boat directly under the apex of the chain and the bow, Lou made contact first with her feet and then lowered herself onto his shoulders with a playful giggle. He let the engine idle in neutral while he eased her down in a slow seductive slide against the front of his body that ended in a sizzling kiss no self-respecting person would engage in while others were watching.

"Dear heaven!" Stella fumed as the outboard revved into gear and they sped away. "And in broad daylight, too!"

"Somebody ought to knock some sense into that girl," Mason growled irritably. "Little flirt – what'd you let her go for, Stuart? Should have made her stay and suffer along with the rest of us."

"Well, I would have," the Captain was still watching the small boat as it receded into the horizon. "Only she's right. She is the best deckhand I got going for me on this trip."

"Who is that kid anyway?" Mason squinted into the sun as if he might be able to tell if he kept looking hard enough. "I've never seen him before."

"Been hanging around the docks the last couple months," Stuart replied. "Does a bit of work with the fleet now and again. Came in on one of them cargo boats before that."

"I wouldn't be surprised if he was the devil's own cousin," Stella pronounced. "And to think she was going to take the baby along!"

"Rather strange he knew right where to find us." The Colonel twisted the top off a bottle of chilled tea and drank half of it down without stopping.

Stella couldn't help thinking how at home he looked in this environment, with his khaki shorts, and Hawaiian shirt hanging loose and unbuttoned to reveal a thatch of curly gray hair. He must have spent a great deal of time at the beach over the years.

"Strange or not," Stuart turned away from the rail and headed back toward his project, "did you see them muscles? I could use a good hand like that on this trip."

"Good Grief!" the Colonel muttered to himself. "Then we'd really have problems to contend with!"

"Two of them acting like that night and day, nobody would miss the movies," Stuart chuckled.

Mason suddenly stood up straighter and shielded his eyes as he tried to catch a last glimpse. "Just what I thought… circling right back to shore."

3

Packing up an apartment was nothing compared to packing up a mansion. Especially one that had been lived in for nearly twenty years. True, very few of the Villa's furnishings actually belonged to Millie, but Stella soon discovered that the latter years of financial troubles had turned her newfound friend into a packrat. Specifically in the food department.

"What in the world!" Stella retied her red bandana to fit more snuggly around her ears as she stood gazing into a wine cellar that was stacked almost to the ceiling with a veritable mountain of food.

"It's my famine chest," Millie explained as she dragged a stack of plastic storage bins up close to the nearest edge. "Left over from our prepper years. Sam was one of those survivalist types that thought World War III was going to break out any day. Either that, or the California coastline was going to drop off into the ocean during the hundred year biggie."

"The hundred year biggie?"

"You know – the big one. The next earthquake that measures over eight points to hit smack along the San Andreas fault. We even have a stash of guns and ammunition in case we ever have to defend ourselves when total chaos breaks loose in the cities."

"Goodness–it must have cost a fortune!"

"Not exactly. Sam was a real wheeler-dealer. Before he left me, we always had plenty of money. Here. You can take half of these bins and start on that end while I get busy on this one."

Stella retreated to her specified area and began to pack can after can of condensed soup and beef stew into the containers. "This hardly looks like your cupboards, Mil… you being such a stickler for cooking fresh from scratch and all."

"In case of a real emergency, there's not

always a working kitchen at hand," Millie explained. "Look at all the people who were stranded in their own front yards after that last big one. Water lines broke. All the power went out. Streets and highways were busted or buckled in so many places you couldn't even drive out."

She stopped for a moment as if remembering and then shook off the memory to get back to work. "Nope. The houses were too dangerous to stay in, so–what with the aftershocks going off for days afterward--most people were stuck camping out in their own front yards with whatever they had on hand in their cupboards. Which this day and age isn't much considering how almost everybody works and eats out most of the time."

"It's true -- hardly anyone cooks at home anymore," Stella agreed. "I had a neighbor back at my old apartment complex who was always dieting, so she didn't want any food around her place at all. Just went to the grocery store every day or so, and ate out every night."

"A lot of people do. Anyway, that's why most of this stuff you can just open up and eat cold right out of the can. Don't have to cook anything and it will last for years."

"Well..." Stella looked in awe at the towering mountain of food that seemed hardly diminished even though they had both been packing it away steadily at their respective ends for the last ten minutes. "All this sure is going to come in handy on the *Dreadful*. So, maybe Sam's survival tendencies weren't such a bad thing after all. And what do you mean he left you? I thought you said he died."

"Before he died he left me." Millie looked at several jars of home-canned something that could either be light gravy or applesauce but had lost the labels. Then packed them into her container, anyway. "Went on a fling with some younger woman and only came back when he found out he was dying."

"Oh. I'm sorry."

"So was I. But I didn't have it in me to turn him away –not after being married twenty-two years. Look here – have you ever tried any of these?" She held up a tan package with black lettering on it. "They're MRE's. You know, military food rations."

"Not hardly. Where did you get so many?"

"From the Colonel. Said he could get more, too."

Stella stopped loading her containers and looked over at Millie. "I thought you said all this was Sam's idea. Oliver's only been here a little over a year, hasn't he?"

"It was Sam's idea to start with. But I'm a firm believer in taking care of myself during a national emergency. You think I'd be like some of those people you see on the news, just sitting around waiting for someone to rescue them? Some even dying? Not me. Not on your life! I'm going to be handing out help, not waiting for it. I never go to the store without bringing back a little something for my famine chest. Force of habit."

"I can see that. But Millie..." Stella straightened up for a moment and put a hand to her aching back. What a long week it had been! "It's obviously been more than could fit into a chest for years. Look at the size of this thing!" She looked up at the pile that nearly touched the ceiling in some places. "There's no way this is all going to fit into that galley pantry, even if

Stuart does move all his paint stuff somewhere else. Shouldn't we prioritize?"

"Mason already built some water-tight crates so we could store the extra down in the hold. Believe me, we're going to need all of it when we find out there isn't a grocery store for a hundred miles up there and we get snowed in until spring in some frozen wilderness."

"Good grief, Millie!" Now, she couldn't help stealing the Colonel's phrase. "Doesn't that thought just send chills up your spine? Surely Mason wouldn't let us all get into such a--"

"He certainly would," her friend informed her. "Mason thinks he can survive anything and figures he can take care of half the rest of the world while he's at it. On account of he was in one of those prison camps during the Vietnam war."

"I didn't know that!" Stella stopped packing again, and looked back over at Millie; this time noticing she had split a seam on the side of her lavender colored pants from so much bending and stretching. "He doesn't seem the type."

"Nobody's that type, believe me. Don't let on to him I told you–he's real touchy about it. But you know what? It's because of that experience we ever met the Colonel. On account of he wanted to use Mason's story in one of the chapters of his hero book. Mase got some kind of medal for something he did back then but I never could get him to show it to me."

"One of Oliver's heroes for a history book--I never would have dreamed! Isn't it rather amazing the way all of us have come together, Mil? I mean, it's almost like … like destiny, or something."

"It's destiny all right. Because while Mase figures it doesn't matter what condition that Alaskan lodge of his is in since we can live under a tree and survive off pine nuts if we have to. But he's going to be pretty darn glad I brought my famine chest along. Plenty of moose and salmon up there, he says. I say nobody wants to live off the same thing for eight months straight, no matter how much the stuff sells for down here in the states. He wouldn't last two weeks without hankering after a pot of my homemade chili, anyway."

"None of the rest of us would, either," Stella pointed out.

"So, get ready for the worst, is what I always say, then celebrate like crazy if nothing happens. Hey--do you realize what time it is, Stel?"

Stella glanced at her watch. "Why, it's three o'clock already, and I'm supposed to meet Oliver downtown at four! We have to get some last minute things for our cabin."

"Better take my car."

"But we might not be back until late."

"Doesn't matter. Mase is coming in to take the last of the stuff aboard and I'll be staying out there from now on. Everything of mine is in, already. Just make sure and lock up the garage when you bring it back, will you? The man who bought it won't be by until Saturday and Lou's picking up a swing shift tonight. Trying to get in all the hours she can before we sail."

"Thanks, Mil!" Stella missed the last words of instruction as she fairly flew up the cellar steps and into the basement.

One more flight of stairs in such a hurry only brought her to the kitchen, and she was already exhausted. How could she possibly clean up and get downtown in time? She certainly couldn't arrive in blue jeans, a checkered blouse and a babushka! Not that Oliver hadn't seen her in the worst of all possible conditions before. It was just that they were planning a farewell dinner at the Luau Palace, since they were practically still on their honeymoon.

Such a thoughtful man she had married… he never ceased to amaze her. Which is why she had no intentions of having him pacing the isles of the curtain department in a store down at the local mall because she completely lost track of time. She had enough shortcomings that would come out sooner or later, and had every intention of making the "honeymoon period" last as long as it possibly could.

So—in a snap decision—she heaved open the iron doors in front of the dumbwaiter and proceeded to climb in. If it had been a good enough elevator for Millie's invalid cousin Gerald all those years, it could certainly get her up to the third story without depleting every ounce of energy she had left. Except there was something in the way.

Several large items, wrapped with brown paper and string, that she could tell the minute she moved them, were paintings. But what were they doing here? Stella didn't have to wonder whether or not they were expensive because every original item in the old Hollywood retreat known as Villa Nofre had been worth a small fortune. Which is why—when curiosity got the better of her—she peeled back a corner of the top frame and peeked inside.

It was that ghastly modern art Millie said she detested, and had packed away into the attic, years ago. Worth a fortune on the right market, though, which she had also told her. Stella counted the frames. Seven of them. Probably the whole collection. Surely they should have been left in the attic with everything else up there for the family of the deceased owner to go through. That is…

Unless Millie had another plan of her own that none of the rest of them knew about.

4

The captain's quarters looked like an entirely different place than the day Stella had her first glimpse of it. Now there were brown plaid drapes at the windows to lend privacy and keep out cold drafts on chilly evenings (Stella loved plaids, they were so homey). A chocolate-colored Berber area rug had been tacked over the old oriental, and a frosted glass globe of Edwardian design (from which the boat actually had its origin) to replace the tasseled lampshade from the bootleg era. Not to mention every inch of the wooden walls had been scrubbed and oiled until they shone like honey.

Her book collection was in place (as if the shelves had been made to exact specifications!), and even the old stove—which now had a warm fire crackling away just to see how it would feel—had been newly blacked and polished over all its nickel trim. There was a new comforter set with matching pillows (browns and plaid) in a lovely little bedroom adjoining the quarters, too. They even had their own private bathroom with a shower.

It should have been heaven.

Instead, Stella sat on the couch (under her favorite rose-colored throw) beneath the Colonel's questioning gaze from where he sat behind the desk (with his writing things all around) and –for the first time– felt uncomfortable in his presence. She was amazed at how quickly she slipped back into her old ways. Like a puzzle piece locking into place, the practice of diverting confrontation by bringing up a shocking but less dangerous subject came as naturally as breathing to her. It always had. Yet, it was not having the same effect on her new husband as it had on the previous one.

"I don't believe it," he finally pronounced. "I just plain don't believe it."

"Do you regret all this then?"

"Stella, I would have married you if you were a hundred and three! Do you really think age has anything to do with it?" He rose up from the desk, unconsciously hiked up the back of his loose-fitting khaki pants, and began to pace.

In spite of the tense moment, she thought how all the rigors of the last few weeks were causing him to shed pounds, and wondered if he shouldn't buy a smaller size. "Looks are deceiving, Oliver. Especially these days." she went on.

"And that's the point!" He turned around just as she was putting the cap back on the coconut oil that had become a nightly ritual to rub onto her face. "Stella--" His tone was imploring. "You can't possibly sit there in those flowered silk pajamas, with that white, Chinese-collar robe thing that practically matches your hair, and expect me to believe you're eighty-one years old! It's ridiculous!"

"Longevity runs in my family."

"Hogwash! Even face lifts and Botox have to be disguised with fancy hairdos and make up. You haven't a thing under that oil but your natural skin."

"Must be the Swedish coming out in me," she mused. "Did I ever tell you my mother's family immigrated to Minnesota from Sweden, Oliver? Way back in… the late eighteen hundreds, I think it was."

He sighed and sat down at the desk, again, so heavily that the leather squeaked under the strain. "After all we've been through, Stel. It's disappointing you feel you have to hide anything from me."

"It isn't as if I made a conscious effort to hide it. It's just that the subject never came up. And now, only because you flipped through my passport."

"It was sitting right here on my desk, where Gerald dropped the mail this morning — both of ours came—I was just taking them out of the envelopes. Besides, that's not the point. I'm talking about whatever it is that's makes you feel it necessary to pass yourself off as someone twenty years older. I already said I don't believe the eighty-one-year-old bit. Not for a minute, I don't."

Stella didn't know what to say about that, so, she didn't say anything.

"Well, I'm sure you'll tell me the real story whenever you feel safe enough. Let's just let it go at that, my dear."

How odd that he should use the word, safe.

"I suppose it's this whirlwind romance of ours." She gave a relieved sigh at having barely avoided catastrophe. "Do you realize I know as little about you as you do me? A military career and you write hero books. That's all I know about you: outside of being divorced and having two grown-up sons you never see—they're so busy off in the military, themselves. Why, for all I know, you could be a… a former inmate of a mental institution."

"Oh, Stella – for crying out loud – don't you think I'd have told you if there were something as serious as that in my past?"

"Not really."

"Well, I would."

Better not go there, then, as that serious omission might give him an even worse shock.

Even though there was a perfectly acceptable explanation if she was ever allowed to explain. "People often try to get others to think differently of them than they actually are," she pointed out. "It doesn't always mean they're hiding something criminal. Take Mason, for instance."

She got to her feet and walked over to push back a shock of gray curls that had fallen onto his forehead. "He lets everyone assume he's nothing more than a self-centered, hard-drinking carpenter, and in reality, he won some sort of Medal of Honor he doesn't want anyone to know about. Imagine being ashamed of a Medal of Honor!"

"Soldiers often feel guilty if they happen to survive when so many of their comrades don't."

She settled comfortably onto his lap and he locked his arms around her waist.

Thank goodness! She didn't think she could stand it if there had been any true rift between them. "And look at Millie. All that fuss about Sam's memory and… they weren't even together until just before he died. He left her for a younger woman."

"Maybe she likes to forget the bad parts and remember it that way, herself."

"My point exactly, dear. Not to mention they were still married the whole time, so it wasn't exactly an untruth, either. Still, it all hit her terribly hard. No money of her own to fall back on. Did you know she spent years squirreling things away for hard times? And not just food, either."

"I take it you saw the famine chest."

"A famine chest I can understand—we should all have one. Hers is a monstrosity but I can understand it. But thc art! Less than two weeks after J.D.—Mr. Willoughby, I mean—so graciously forgave her for selling off all that other stuff, too. There's no way she could be trading it in to pay electricity and repair bills, anymore. Where could she cash something that famous in where it wouldn't be found out? If I didn't know better, I'd say she had an entirely different plan for herself. One that doesn't include the rest of us. You know, I don't even think Gerald knows—and he's her cousin. Nobody does."

"What art?"

"All those famous modern art pictures I found in the dumbwaiter, this afternoon. The only reason I saw them is because I was late and needed a ride up instead of climb those hundreds of stairs. And there they were! All wrapped in brown paper and tied up with string—ready to mail. You don't do that just to move something to another room or leave in a closet. And they certainly aren't to decorate her cabin on the *Dreadful*, either."

"*Dreadnaught*, Stell. You know how it physically pains Stuart to hear you call it that."

"It's a much more fitting name, if you ask me."

"Try thinking about it as our gateway to adventure. By the time this trip is over, I'm sure we'll be almost as attached to it as Stuart is. Look how our Captain's quarters spruced up so well."

"Oh, they did! You know I was almost envious of everyone else moving aboard before we did? I'm that fond of all this, already. I thought Millie was, too. She did tell me those pictures were worth a fortune, though. Then again, maybe she had second thoughts about leaving them in an empty house and decided to send them to the family directly. Do you think that's what it was?"

"That sounds a lot more like our Millie than absconding with them. Remember how upset she got at the prospect of going to jail? She probably just forgot about the paintings in all this confusion of moving. What do you want to bet she'll remember them halfway through Canada somewhere, and then fuss about it all the way to Alaska."

"You're probably right."

"We'll ask her."

"Which is entirely possible because we've all worked ourselves into a stupor this week, trying to keep up with Stuart. I wonder why the first thing we do, when anything doesn't seem quite right, is to think the absolute worst of people? I wouldn't be surprised if the whole thing turned out to be--"

The familiar strains of the Marine Band piped up from his shirt pocket, and Stella got up to put another log on the fire while he answered the phone.

"Henry, here. Oh, hello, Mason. Not back yet? No, just Stella and I. Villa looked all dark and locked up when we put the car back in the garage. Didn't even go in."

Stella stopped poking at the fire and turned around in time to see the Colonel's gray eyebrows scrunch together into his thinking expression. "Course we will. Be there as soon as we can."

She felt a tightening in her chest. "Now, what happened?"

"Millie isn't at the house, and it's been over an hour since she was supposed to meet Mason there." He got to his feet and slipped the phone back into his pocket in one smooth motion. "Not answering her phone, either."

5

What could only be called a "wild goose chase" ensued. Stella threw some clothes on over her pajamas, and rode back across the bay with the Colonel and Stuart (who was driving all out), to search for Millie. By that time Mason was an exhausted wreck, having called every emergency room in town, thinking her heart condition may have got the better of her somewhere with all the stresses and strains of the move. Then he single-handedly began a search of all nooks and cupboards in the mansion from the attic down.

By the time the others arrived, he had reached the kitchen on the main level.

Stella forced herself not to think the worst and hurried off to search on her own. But what

Millie had told her earlier about being stranded in the frozen north, hundreds of miles from grocery stores (maybe even electricity!), she certainly wouldn't blame her if she decided to go live back east with one of her children, after all. True, each of them had been sincere about sticking together. Especially after discovering what their individual prospects would be, should they all have to fend for themselves separately. All of them agreed they were more than capable of pooling their resources and living the same way they had here at the Villa, somewhere else. But Alaska?

To some place Mason had acquired in a card game, sight unseen.

Why, the only reason Stella wasn't quaking in her own boots, right now, was because it would be a grand adventure just getting there. Sort of an extended honeymoon. And if things turned out too badly, she and the Colonel still had enough money to rent something small to get by on. But the others didn't. And considering how attached they had all become she hadn't thought twice about not pitching in.

The truth was, pitching in for this little misfit family was beginning to change her life. It had brought her out of some of her own thin places and she had no desire to go back to those, again. She couldn't go back! Which was why she wanted to have a private talk with Millie, in case she really was thinking of desertion. They had to stick together!

If they didn't, the whole thing could turn into a disaster and nobody would succeed.

She was thinking of all these things as she headed down to the wine cellar (whether by premonition, or it was simply the last place she had seen Millie), and threw back the latch on the door. Even though it was impossible to accidentally lock oneself inside and her friend could only have latched it if she had come out.

Which was exactly how Stella discovered an unconscious Millie, draped over a row of plastic bins, as if someone had conked her on the head. Something that proved false, as did a heart attack. In the end, it seemed the heavy door had somehow closed on its own, and – after realizing her cell phone wouldn't work in a place that could have doubled as a fallout shelter in case of World War III—she proceeded to console herself in the emergency liquor supply while waiting to be rescued.

Something that could happen to anybody, especially if they were claustrophobic.

Still, with one problem after another faced and solved by the increasingly brave band of adventurers, they did actually manage to sail out of the protected southern California bay, three days later.

It was a glorious spring day, the sea was calm, and the *Dreadnaught* behaved beautifully. So beautifully that the trip seemed charmed. So, it was no wonder, after ten days of worry-free voyaging (they even did several stints of night-traveling because the moon and stars were bright and spectacular), and only brief stops in San Francisco and Portland, they finally ended up anchored off Vancouver, Canada, to show their passports and wait for a border inspection to proceed north.

Captain Stuart did everything by the book. In fact, he had made this run several times in his working days (on more modern vessels but the course was the same), and left his little group of passengers to rest and relax on board while he collected all their passports and set out to take care of business. All of which went through without a hitch. Even during the long and thorough inspection. After that, a few hours of sight-seeing and the purchase of a few last-minute items, and they were soon on their way, again.

It was a very long way to Alaska.

However, the coast of British Columbia is a wild one, with long stretches of wilderness, and weather that can change as fast as one's feelings. There were a few mornings they woke up enveloped by a thick fog (that Stuart referred to as a "pea souper"), and had to wait until it lifted to continue their journey. Something that had little effect on the happy group. Whether it was because of the marvelous sea air, or the fact they had enough supplies on board to get by for an entire year if they had to, no one knew.

Because, not only were they all getting along splendidly, they had become quite comfortable (and proficient) in their respective "sea duties." Even Stuart had to admit the voyage was turning out to be one of the best he had ever made. Mostly because of the food. With three women aboard who loved cooking, the meals were fabulous. He even started to contemplate the possibilities of taking on a few charters after this trip was over, in order to complete renovations.

But all that was before their first storm.

Up till that point, most of the travel had been motoring. Outside a time or two of raising the sails (in order to keep up skills, as Stuart put it), the entire trip, so far, had felt like nothing short of a delightful holiday cruise. For everybody.

Even Gerald, who took his "turn at the wheel" with the utmost seriousness and respect, was actually becoming dependable. He stayed precisely on course, did exactly what the Captain told him at all times, and was even getting a bit of color back into his face. Of course, he had to make a few concessions, considering his condition. He rarely left the main deck (where his cabin was situated), and—except for the few steps up to the wheelhouse—avoided stairs and companionway ladders, altogether.

He was cold most of the time, too, but solved that problem by wearing a black navy watch cap (both waking and sleeping), as well as half a multicolored Mexican poncho that was cut off at elbow-length so that he could still do his work. Something that made him resemble the haggard form of Lincoln, moving through hallways of the White House, during the last dark days of the Civil War. Without the beard, and should you come up on him from behind.

However, that part of sea—which funnels through the straits from the "big water" (as Stuart called it) outside the islands—can turn suddenly wild and dangerous with hardly any warning. And considering they had known nothing but idyllic conditions the entire way, all hands were caught horrifically unaware when one of those famous storms crashed into them. That is, all accept Captain Stuart.

Who knew exactly what to do in such conditions, if he only had at least one person who could lift more than fifty pounds in a full gale. He hoped everyone else could handle at least twenty and still manage to stay on their feet. This because the sea was so rough the engine propellers were out of the water half the time, and the old schooner was much more stable with her sails up than without them. After all, it was what she had been designed for.

Meanwhile, everyone except the Captain was seasick. Not counting the baby, who was never bothered by anything, and having a delightful time bouncing wildly, back and forth, in his "Johnny Jumper" attached to a cabin ceiling as he watched his "Uncle Gerald" throw up into a bucket. His mother and Mason were out on deck, doing their level-best at hauling the mainsail up, as Stella and Millie grappled with "taking up the slack" in the sheets.

This so Stuart could see to the sudden banging noises that were coming from his engine, and the Colonel—by sheer size and strength—struggled with the wheel to keep their ship bucking through the waves instead of getting trapped in the troughs between. All of which presented itself to Stella (even though she was scared-stiff, and wet to the bone in spite of rain-gear) as such a display of courage and cooperation that she would remember it for the rest of her life.

One particular scene, especially.

It was the expression on the Colonel's face (when she looked up at him through the wheelhouse window) after the mainsail suddenly tore in half and began flapping like thunder, causing the lines to go slack, and send them tumbling toward the rail when the boat began to roll. With the determination of a weight-lifter contending for Olympic gold, he clamped onto the wheel and began to inch the giant hull back up by brute force, in order to save them from shipwreck.

But it wasn't enough.

***

At the same time, down in the engine room, the Captain knew exactly what was happening, topside, by the way his vessel made the sudden roll to starboard and sent him crashing into the bulkhead. Now, they had it, he thought to himself, because not one of them up there knew what to do next. "Haul up that jib!" he hollered, even though no one could hear him from down there. "Get some way on before we lose her in this--"

BOOM! There was the loud bang of rigging as the boat wallowed over onto her other side, caught in the steep trough between waves. Which gave him a decision to make. Take the few minutes to replace the broken belt and get the engine going, again, or leave it to dash topside, and pull the foresails up so the boat would at least have enough steerage not to founder. "God help me!" he cried, heaving himself to his feet. "I'm at sea with a bunch of idiots!"

It was at that moment a dark form darted past him and he distinctly heard, "Fix the belt--I got the sails!" in a tone of such confidence that his old Navy days kicked back in, and he found himself "snapping to" without so much as a care who it was.

He only knew he had a bona fide seaman aboard, after all, and a flood of relief washed over him. In the nick of time, too. Then it occurred to him he had never had such immediate attention from the Almighty in his entire life. Something which led to the disturbing conclusion that, either an angel had just passed by, or…

The *Dreadnaught* had gone down, already, and he was about to meet his maker.

6

A tumult of thoughts ran through Stella's mind during those moments. It wasn't the first time she had faced death, but it was the first time she had ever been able to stand up to that terror with such peace and utter clarity. What happened next played out before her in a sort of dreamlike slow motion, giving her plenty of time to react.

The first thing she did was to grab hold of Millie as she tumbled by, and pull her to the safety of the rail, where she could hold on. Then as the boat began to roll in the opposite direction, she felt the line she had dropped begin to whistle away over her feet, and picked it up. Just in time to wind it around a nearby cleat (why, she had never managed the task that fast before!) and stop the free-swinging boom from plowing into Mason, who had his back to it, trying to tie off from the other side. Disaster avoided. Almost like a miracle.

Which is just what she was thinking when she saw the dark stranger come running past her, right out onto the bowsprit that hung over all those wildly tossing waves. He peeled the canvas back with quick agility on yet another sail that was stashed there, and began hauling it up the stays. Only to be stopped by a tangle of tattered mainsail that had wound itself round the thick wire, about a third of the way up when the big one had torn loose.

"Lou!" called a familiar masculine voice. "Ninja ladder!"

The girl was beside him in an instant, and what Stella saw next was amazing.

He bent down long enough for her to climb up onto his shoulders and grab hold of the bunched up sail, in order to pull herself along the wire as he slowly stood up, again. Still standing on his shoulders when she reached the place the tattered pieces were wrapped around, he snatched a knife from his belt and handed it up to her.

The wire was attached at the top of the foremast, slanting down at an angle to the very tip of the bow. Another miracle. If the obstruction had been any higher, she wouldn't have been able to reach it. As it was she had the offending tatters cut away and was back on deck in a mere few moments.

At which point, Cole DeForio (Stella recognized him the minute Lou Edna climbed up and down over him with such confidence and familiarity), quickly finished hauling up the large jib sail, while Mason pulled the trailing line attached to it around a nearby winch-drum and tied it off. The boat immediately headed back up into the wind, and regained enough control for the Colonel to have steerage, again.

They were saved!

Less than five minutes after that the engine sputtered back to life, and the *Dreadnaught* continued to plow steadily through the storm toward the nearest harbor, where they could drop anchor and wait the thing out. A place not far off from Alert Bay (which was not on their list of official stops), and not a sign of civilization was in sight. But it was well protected and safe. And more welcoming to the exhausted adventurers than any waterfront town could have been.

The young couple disappeared immediately after they got there, giving everyone else time to collect themselves and their thoughts, down in the galley. They all needed to recuperate before the inevitable confrontation. At the very least, there was a lot of explaining to do.

"I take back every critical thing I've said about Shortcake," said Mason, holding one of the large mugs of hot bullion Millie was handing out to everyone who meandered in after changing into dry clothes. "Any girl who will hop-to like that in an emergency is all right by me."

"She lied to us, again, Mason." The Colonel was not one to give quarter to dishonesty. "Been hiding that young man, all along. Where--I have no idea--considering how thoroughly those officials went over this boat when we came through customs. Imagine what could happen if they had found a stowaway."

"I shudder to think about it," agreed Stella (another narrow escape!). She was sitting next to him at the table, wearing a matching knit hat and scarf (periwinkle blue), with her still-chilled hands hugging her own mug of bullion. Would she ever be truly warm, again?

"When you're in love you do crazy things," said Millie.

"When you're in love you aren't ashamed of it," Mason added. "So, he must be in some kind of trouble. Again."

"So…" The Colonel took a deep breath. "We've been smuggling a criminal through Canada."

This just as Gerald dragged in, still somewhat wobbly, and so pale Millie immediately poured a large splash of brandy into his bullion before handing it to him. "Better sit down before you fall down, Gerry," she whispered.

"E-gads…" He sank onto the seat beside Stella. "Lou didn't bring any drugs aboard, did she?"

"Of course not!" huffed Millie. "She's too

good a mother to get wrapped up in that stuff. Look how she quit drinking the minute she found out she was pregnant. And she's as loyal as my own daughter, too. In her own way."

"We could sit here guessing, all day." Mason got to his feet. "Let's get them in here and talk, so we can decide what's the best thing to do."

"Can't see as there is a best thing," said the Colonel. His cheeks were growing rosy from the warmth of the stove. Then again, he did have a bit more insulation than everyone else, with all those extra pounds turning to muscle, Stella mused. "Wouldn't be right to dump him off in a foreign country," he went on, "and he definitely did the right thing when he had to."

"Dump who off?" Gerald handed his empty mug back toward Millie (who had just bent down to re-twist the yellow towel she had wrapped around her wet hair), and knocked it out of his hand against her hip, instead. "Tell Stuart I need a little more time, Mil—I'm doing my level best!"

"Not you, Gerald. Our stowaway. Lou smuggled Cole DeForio, aboard, and now we're all accomplices." She snatched up the mug and refilled it, again.

"E-gads!" he replied, and took it.

At which point, Mason returned with the contrite young couple following behind, whose youthful good looks seemed absolutely striking in contrast to their bedraggled elders. Lou Edna's blonde hair was gathered into a band at the nape of her neck, she hadn't a speck of make-up on, and she was beautiful.

"Well, it was a snap decision," she began before anyone even asked them a question. "There were some bad people after him and I had no choice."

"One always has a choice," said the Colonel. "There are other ways to help besides breaking more laws."

"Let's get something straight, right off." Cole met the Colonel's gaze and pointed to his own chest for emphasis. "I wasn't the one who broke the law."

"Do you have a passport or don't you?" Mason asked him.

"To begin with I didn't break any laws," the young man corrected himself. "Like she said, it was a snap decision. I just didn't have enough time to get one."

"Bad people aren't usually interested in border regulations. What's Shortcake talking about, here?"

"It was me that talked him into it, Pop. I told him we could get good money at pawn shops for those pictures."

"What pictures?" asked Millie.

"The crazy art collection."

"What?"

"E-gads, Lou..." Gerald moaned. "The ones painted by E.J.'s first wife? They'd be worth a small fortune at *Christie's*, by now How much did you sell them for?"

"Nothing, they disappeared."

"After she spent the money they already gave us for a down payment, too." Cole wiped a trickle of water off the side of his face that was coming from his wet hair. "You don't cross those kind of people. They'll come after you for stealing peanuts."

"Those kind of people don't usually do payments," Mason said.

"They paid seven hundred and fifty dollars,

based on the preliminary artist sketches," Lou informed them. "The ones in that portfolio. I needed some things for the trip if we're going to be gone so long. You know I spent a hundred and fifty just in diapers? Then baby food and—a bunny suit, of course. Three of them, in fact. The Senator's crawling around so much, now, he's got one wore out, already."

"Don't change the subject," said Mason. "We all know how money disappears."

Millie sat down on the other side of the table, next to Mason, with a heavy sigh. "You should have asked us, Lou. Those paintings weren't ours to sell. After everything J.D. did for us, too."

"But you said yourself they were garbage, Mil. And the whole place was going to be knocked down, anyway. I didn't think anybody would even notice."

"They weren't our things."

"Wrong's wrong, even if it helps you" quoted Gerald, before he got up to refill his mug, again. "You got taken on the sketches, too. They'd have brought a strong five thousand at auction."

"Yeah, well I don't happen to know any fancy art collectors," Cole pointed out. "And, by that time we were in a hurry."

"You're lucky you didn't let go of the paintings or we'd all be in a fix." Mason rubbed a hand over his unshaved chin. "Long as they're back at the house, we're safe. I'll deal with J.D. about the sketches. He's reasonable enough."

There was such a long silence that he glanced around the entire table. Now, everyone looked guilty. "They are at the *Villa*… right?"

"Pop…" Lou Edna shook her head in disbelief. "They just… disappeared! We looked everywhere for them!"

"What? Holy--" BOOM! His fist banged down with a resounding thump. "This whole situation's getting worse by the minute!"

"Hold on, Mase." The Colonel raised his hand to interrupt the outburst. "It just so happens Stella found them."

Such a unanimous exclamation of relief burst forth from everyone at the same time, it sounded staged. Except for Stella. She tried nudging the Colonel under the table but he spoke out too soon.

"I found them, all right," she finally confessed. "They were in the dumbwaiter."

"That's right where I hid them but they weren't there when we went back. Those guys were waiting for us and when we didn't show up, they kept calling. They said they were coming over to deal with us. We had to lock Millie in the cellar, too, because I just didn't have enough time to explain."

"You know I almost had a heart attack down there?" Millie accused. "I was in there for hours!"

"But you were out by the time we got back," the girl reasoned.

"A lot of this is my fault, "said Stella. "You see, I had a bit of extra time before we moved onto the boat and mailed them off to the pawn shop they were addressed to. As a favor to Millie because her return address was on there."

Now, a unanimous gasp of horror escaped everybody.

"My pills!" Millie reached into the pocket of her pink housecoat, in search of them. "My heart pills! Oh, Mase—I'm going to faint!"

"Wait!" This time, it was Lou Edna who raised her hand. "It's OK—it's OK! Oh, this is all too funny!" She leaned her head back to indulge in a moment of nervous laughter. "If you mailed them just the way they were, we're OK!"

"You have the weirdest sense of humor, Lou." Cole got up and poured himself a cup of coffee, realized it wasn't coffee, and poured it down the sink, instead. "I've never felt this stupid in my life and we still have major problems, here."

"J.D.'s going to be wondering where those pictures are!" Millie complained. "I gave him our forwarding address, too." She moaned at her own stupidity. "Now, when they turn up on the black market somewhere, any investigator with half a brain will be able to trace things back to me. The real crooks will get away, scot-free, and I could end up in women's prison, after all! Lou—how could you do this to me!"

"I didn't do anything that bad, Millie. I addressed them to *Peabody's Peculiar Treasures*—J.D.'s antique place—not the pawn shop we were dealing with. In case you found them in the dumbwaiter before we could actually make the deal. Didn't want to give you another heart attack."

"You mean, I didn't send them to the mafia, after all?" Stella was so relieved she leaned her forehead against the Colonel's shoulder and sighed. "Oh, thank heaven!"

"Mr. Peabody's probably had them for days, now," the girl assured. "So—other than harboring an illegal alien--"

"Oh, Lou Edna!" Millie dropped her face into her hands. "If you aren't the death of me one of these days, I will be a lucky woman!"

"Shortcake, we can handle." Mason jerked a thumb toward Cole. "It's him we got to figure out what to do with, now."

"I'll tell you what we're gonna do with him!" The booming voice of Captain Stuart echoed from the companionway leading down to the engine room. He ducked smartly into the galley, with his hair all slicked back, and a clean shirt on. It had a small rip at the left shoulder, and only smelled faintly of diesel.

"Yeah, I knew this was coming sooner, or

later, so…" Cole stood up straighter and looked him in the eye. "Let's have it, Old Man."

"You're promoted to First Mate."

"Are you kidding me?"

"You will remain aboard this vessel—without shore leave—all the way to Alaska. Where you will immediately apply for a passport. And the rest of you…"

Stuart looked them all over with a warm appreciation shinning in his eyes, and pronounced, "Are hereby released from idiot-status. By the Almighty—you performed like regular sailors, out there. Every last one of you!"

7

That night, as Stella sat tucked beneath her rose- colored throw reading before a pleasantly crackling fire, it suddenly occurred to her how far they had all come, working together as a team. Why it had literally saved them! And—without the many miracles she was so sure she had experienced that day—they could all be dead. In fact, she was beginning to feel like something of a cat with nine lives, lately, the way she had been escaping so many disasters.

Now, here she was in her safe little home, in this quiet harbor, halfway to Alaska. Could it be that God truly cared for her—in a personal way—and took a "divine hand" in all things concerning her? Why, if that were true... a person could do just about anything. An ordinary person would be capable of doing extraordinary things.

Maybe even great things.

All at once, an incredible sense of peace and contentment settled over her. She wondered if it wasn't truly the most wonderful feeling she had ever experienced. What's more, for the first time in her entire life, she had someone to share it with. A person who understood such things. She looked over to where the Colonel was working away contentedly on his next book of heroes.

"Oliver?"

"Yes, my dear?" he replied without looking up right away. Stella loved it when he got involved in his work. His face went through so many different expressions it was almost like watching a movie.

"I just thought you might like to know something." He looked over at her then. "Yes?"

"I'm sixty-three."

"I thought so, Stel. You know that's just

what I thought? It's a wonder they don't ask you to prove it whenever you renew your driver's license. It really is."

"When you have white hair, that's all anyone really notices about you."

"Hmm." He drummed his fingers lightly on the arm of his chair, as if thinking. "Anything else you want to tell me about all that?"

"Not at the moment." There would be plenty of time to tell him about those other things. She would tell him little by little. And—who knows—in the telling, maybe she would have more of this peace and contentment to fill her life. And less of those visions like that lady standing at the stove. Where did such things come from?

"You know, my dear..." He suddenly closed down his laptop and gave her his full attention. "Everyone has something to hide. Every last one of us. Look at Cole and Lou Edna. The lengths they went to pull this whole thing off. And all for seven- hundred and fifty dollars, that made them feel worthless inside."

"You have to admit it was clever the way they managed it, though," she said. Stella knew what it was like to be forced into desperate decisions and then end up in a worse place because of them. "Her dropping him off in the rowboat on the American side, late at night when we were all asleep, and then bringing him over the next night, again, after the inspection. He's been aboard all this time and not a one of us had a clue."

"Yes, and if they would put that much effort toward honest work, they'd have more than enough respect to live on by now. Along with everything else that comes from doing what's right."

"Maybe they will, after all this." Stella closed her book and smiled. "He was certainly surprised when he got promoted to First Mate! Did you see the look on his face? It was like that was the first decent thing anybody ever did for him in his entire life."

"Wouldn't be surprised if it was. For sure he'll turn out to be the best hand Stuart's ever had. Wait and see."

"I hope so."

"They'll have a strong bond between them, too. I could see it's begun already. It's what comes of sharing something of yourself that gets met with acceptance and fair judgment from others. On the other hand, hidden things eat away at you a bit at a time, over a long period of time. It's one of the best forms of destruction there is."

Stella thought that was probably a good lead-in to tell him her own story. But it had been such a long and trying day. An extreme of highs and lows. The Colonel was right, of course. She knew it in her heart as soon as he said those words. But just as she was contemplating whether or not she was even up to such an ordeal, he smiled that wonderful smile of his.

"No need to speak of it any more, tonight, Stel. We have all the time in the world." He answered the question as if she had spoken it out loud. "Besides that, we start with ourselves. Just put ourselves in God's hands, and let him reveal what we need to change, a bit at a time. Somewhere along the line we become more transparent with everyone else, too. And one day we may just wake up and realize we are actually starting to resemble God, Himself. 'From glory to glory,' as the scriptures tell us. Just by watching what He does for us every day. Looking for it, even."

"Sounds wonderful when you put it that way, Oliver. Changing for the better, I mean."

"It's a miracle, my dear... an out and out miracle!"

"I will bring the blind by a way that they knew not... I will make darkness light before them, and crooked things straight. These things will I do... and not forsake them."

Isaiah 42:16

Author's Note

Benjamin Franklin, who was quoted at the beginning of this story, was a man who threw in his lot with others, against impossible odds, many different times during his life.

Difficulties that were overcome not so much because he was a good businessman, an avid scientist and inventor, or even an amazing diplomat. But because, as he said, "Our prayers, Sir, were heard, and they were graciously answered. All of us who were engaged in the struggle must have observed frequent instances of a Superintending providence in our favor."

I find it interesting during research, to discover how much those who do great things seemed to have been "divinely prepared" beforehand. Benjamin Franklin is a good example of this. Even though he was born into a large working-class family (one of the youngest of seventeen children), and had to be apprenticed into a trade at the age of twelve, he was raised by Puritan parents, and eventually settled in Philadelphia: that productive "experimental city" established under the Quaker influence of William Penn. The “city of brotherly love.”

I also found it interesting that Franklin did his most important—and most difficult—work after the age of seventy. In his famous autobiography, he put together a list of personal “virtues” he lived by that he felt were vital to his success, especially in working with others. You can find this short, easy- to-read ebook, for free, at many places online.

I feel richer for having read it, myself.

About Lilly Maytree

Lilly Maytree is the author of *Gold Trap, The Pandora Box,* and *The Stella Madison Capers*. Books that sent her careening along on her "Mystery Tours" with her captain husband aboard the *Glory B.* She loves sharing these adventures with readers. It has even been said that she time-travels (but that's probably just a rumor). To find out about her current adventures, simply visit:

www.LillyMaytree.com

Other Books by
Lilly Maytree

Novels...

Gold Trap

Megan Jennings is headed to Africa for high adventure and divine appointments until she makes a small wrong turn. But what is faith, if not to strike out against impossible odds believing you will win? Or leap out into the dark knowing someone will be there to catch you? Someone does catch her... but it isn't who she was expecting.

The Pandora Box

Journalist D.J. Parker learns the location of a famous cache of diamonds that were stolen during World War II. What she doesn't know is—the federal government has been following the case for years. With an old journal to lead the way, she sets out aboard a yacht that once carried the infamous Herman Goering. A thrilling treasure hunt that could either prove to be the adventure of a lifetime... or her worst nightmare.

The Stella Madison Capers...

Home Before Dark

(Caper #1)

Here is the first of the Stella Madison Capers, the story of how everything started, and how she escaped from a catastrophe that seemed to come out of nowhere. Which is the nature of catastrophes but it's so hard to be logical when you're in the middle of one. It's also the story of how she met the colonel (if you're interested in that sort of thing).

A Thief in the House

(Caper #2)

Stella Madison is back, this time with a bevy of friends. But just how far should a person go when it comes to sticking by their friends? There's a thief in the rambling old mansion she moved into. And while it was someone who was quick to lend help when Stella needed it most, how can she possibly return the favor without jeopardizing herself along with them? No person is obligated to go that far... right?

Voyage of the Dreadnaught

collection of four Stella Madison Capers

Here is a collection of the four Stella Madison Capers covering the entire voyage of the Dreadnaught, through the Inside Passage to Alaska. Includes: *Sea Trials, The Pushover Plot*, *Lost in the Wilderness*, and *The Last Resort*. Also includes a brief account of Lilly Maytree's true-life voyage along the same route, in the sailboat *Glory B*.

For Writers...

Unspoken Rules

Popular books (those stories everyone likes no matter what the subject) all have certain things in common. And what they have most in common is what they DON'T do. Within the following pages, dear writer, you will find the three most important "don'ts" of popular fiction that I learned when I was studying the masters. Why? Because I love research and I never mind sharing my notes.

Writing Rules!

(a mysterious student handbook)

A mysterious little desktop handbook that can help anyone (well, almost anyone) with writing rules. Especially if you are a student and have to write things all the time.

For Parents...

Behave Yourself!

Teaching your children to discipline themselves.

Are you tired of bickering during daily routines encroaching on way too much of your family time? Here is a book that offers a two-week program that teaches your children to discipline themselves. Hard to believe? Here are the step-by-step secrets of how it's done, and why it works.

The Nature of Children

(And how to deal with it.)

A manual based on a compilation of parenting articles Lilly wrote over several years as a columnist for Childcare Magazine. It is a result of many requests from parents for more information about that content and the foundation of the methods she used both in raising her own children, and in her classrooms.

After years of experience, she has a lot to say about what motivates children and has implemented many of her unique ideas into books and programs that others can use.

For an autographed copies, visit:

www.LillyMaytree.com

Excerpt from

The Pushover Plot

Stella Madison Caper #4

Lilly Maytree

To those who have had to contend with the darker side of supernatural—may you never be left there.

"A lie that is half-truth is the darkest of all lies." *Alfred Tennyson*

1

Stella Madison walked down the long dark hallway and deliberately ignored the flutter of fear it gave her. It was ridiculous, really, considering how many others were nearby who wouldn't hesitate to respond to any call for help. Then a regular jolt replaced that flutter because she suddenly remembered how often her own fears had robbed her of her voice in the most desperate hours. Something which made her revert to the old childhood trick of darting from safety to safety as fast as she possibly could.

So, having left the warm comfort at the side of her sleeping husband, she veered toward what had originally been known as the First Mate's cabin, to listen for the deep, reassuring snores of Mason Jeffries. Then to the faint sliver of light shining beneath Gerald's door (who still slept with a light on to "orient himself" even though they had all been aboard the *Dreadnaught* for nearly a month). After that, it was only a hop and a skip to the galley, where Millie left a light on over the stove in case anyone should get hungry in the middle of the night and come looking for a snack.

In fact, she began to hear somebody moving around in there as she got closer, along with the distinctly delicious smell of *Ovaltine* (why, she hadn't tasted any of that in years!). Evidence that someone beside herself hadn't been able to sleep, either. How nice it would be to enjoy a quiet chat instead of wading through the predawn hour all alone. Millie needing to take one of her pills, maybe, or Lou, up with the baby for some reason. Although if it was Captain Stuart, she probably wouldn't stay long as he was about the oddest person she had ever known. Not counting mentally deranged people which she had seen more than her share of.

Funny how memories from so long ago

came suddenly to mind at certain times.
"I guess I'm not the only one who couldn't sleep," she spoke quietly as she pushed through the door, so as not to startle whoever it was. Only no one answered. Instead, she caught just a glimpse of someone disappearing through the companionway door on the far side of the sailboat's galley that led down to below decks. Someone in a full-length, light-colored gown and a dark braid that hung halfway down their back.

Stella got goosebumps when she saw that because none of the *Dreadnaught*'s crew had hair that long. She reached for the corner of the large iron stove to steady herself but got even more of a fright to discover it was stone cold. No one had been heating any hot chocolate in here. Maybe it had been another stowaway. Considering all the dark nooks and crannies in this vessel and how many weeks Lou Edna had managed to hide her young man without a one of them having the slightest idea... it was a possibility.

A better one than the alternative, anyway.

Besides, how could those terrible things be

happening, again, when she was cured of all that so long ago? Especially when her wonderful new life had just begun. They couldn't be! There simply had to be another explanation.

She pulled open the narrow cupboard next to the stove where they kept all the hot drink supplies, and began to rummage through. Teas, coffee, hot cider, bouillon, hot chocolate... but no *Ovaltine.* That distinct mixture of malt in it was unmistakable. A realization that turned the cozy galley intimidating and made her want nothing more than to hurry back to where she belonged.

Along with another urge to have that talk with the colonel about her not-so-ordinary past that she kept putting off. In a few quick steps she was pushing back through the door, again, but only to collide with what looked like an old woman wrapped in a shawl, fairly gliding down the shadowy companionway.

At the same time Stella toppled backward, a distinctly male voice hollered, "Away, you foul spirit!" before tripping right over the top of her and landing hard on the other side. Along with an empty mug and sauce pan that clattered across the floorboards. "What—what? Good grief! Stella! Is it really you?"

"Of course, it's me! That's an awful thing to call someone, Gerry."

"What are you—doing—wandering around this time of night in that—that whatever it is?"

"It's my white terry with a Chinese collar." She got to her feet, feeling rather silly now that someone else was there. "I'm not going to say what I thought you were, with that cut-in-half serape you always wear on top of everything."

"I detest being cold, and the rest got in the way of my arms." He took the hand she offered, to get himself up off the floor. "Sorry for the name-calling. But— blast!" It was part of a Captain Stuart phrase (after a month at sea, they were all talking like old salts), "You scared the daylights out of me! Took you for another one of those ghastly apparitions."

"You mean, you actually saw one?"

"One? They're all over the place around here. Getting so a man can't even hot up his *Ovaltine* without running into the things."

So, she did smell *Ovaltine*! Stella laughed

out of sheer relief. "You don't know how glad I am to hear that. But the stove's cold, how did you do it?"

"Have a hotplate in my room but no sink. And I don't find anything in the least funny about it. All this rot, it's—it's serious business." He pushed the black watch-cap farther back on his head and then picked up his dishes. "Makes me rue the day I ever went gallivanting after such stuff. If I only knew then what I know now!"

"I'm sorry, Gerry. I wasn't making fun. I just had sort of a scare, myself. I'm glad it was you I ran into and not... something else."

"Yes, well... I must say, it's things like this that made it necessary to switch my major to botany from Medieval history, if you want to know the truth."

"I thought you told me your degree was in archeology." They went back through the cabin-way door into the galley. "Even said you taught a few semesters of it at the junior level. Remember?"

"I was, originally. However, it was worse

than the Medieval, what with all those curs-ed artifacts we were forever digging up. Didn't like it at all after I'd finished. And the thought of spending so many hours in dusty museum basements, cleaning and cataloging them... well, they were as bad as the castles—worse even. Then, again, it might have just been me. Now, I actually think the things followed me over from England. That's where I first opened the door to them, anyway."

"The apparitions?"

"Seems like it. I tell you, that whole castle study was a nightmare. Never even finished out the class."

"I don't blame you. There's nothing worse than being scared out of your wits." Then she corrected herself. "Other than being dead, altogether."

"Sometimes I think I might as well be, the way it's ruined my life." He turned on the water at the sink in the far corner to rinse out his things, and the soft whir of the water pump went on. "Oh, and that bosh about them not being able to travel over water? Isn't true. Not one bit. It's been ten times worse since I came home." "You mean, you're not Millie's cousin from England? Then why do you talk that way?" Stella was beginning to wonder if Gerald might be one of those compulsive liars, that you couldn't believe a word from. Or, a mentally unstable type that could have been helped in hospitals but never qualified for the programs because they weren't dangerous. The kind more easily controlled with medication. He did take an unbelievable amount of pills every day.

"Oh, we're cousins, all right. Born and raised in the same town. But it's a... well, it's a fake accent." He glanced over at her with a slight apologetic smile, just enough to show the space between his two front teeth. "Started when I went to college. You know, to impress people. Now, I can't quit."

"It's more old English than modern, you know. I keep expecting you to burst out with "forsooth!" or something."

"Or, dastardly," he added, "It's true, I do like the old phrases best. Always have. I like to think I was born out of time, except—with the high infant mortality back then—I probably wouldn't have made it past the age of three. Rate I'm going, now isn't much better, though. Putting up with all this when I'm hardly past fifty."

"You attribute some of your physical ailments to these...um... apparitions, too?"

"Mostly. The shaking, the weakness, insomnia... that sort of thing."

Stella gave a thoughtful sigh and sat down on the tufted burgundy cushions (that were a bit threadbare and oil-stained) surrounding the dining area. "I've been seeing an apparition, too, Gerry," she suddenly confessed. "I thought it was all in my mind. Hallucinations, or something. But two people can't both be having the same hallucinations. Right?"

"Highly unlikely." He came over to sit across from her, still drying his hands on a blue dishtowel. "What have you been doing to get rid of yours? We should compare notes."

"I never knew you could get rid of them. I thought they just happened."

"Of course you can get rid of them. Or, so I've heard. There's a whole theological philosophy about that. Haven't had any luck with it, myself, yet, but I've only just started trying. Meanwhile, mind telling me how you cope?"

"Cope with what?"

"How you deal with it all. You know, the ugliness, the torment, and—"

"The what?"

"And the out-and-out filth!"

"Good heavens!" She shuddered at the very thought. "I haven't seen anything as terrible as all that! Only a lovely middle-aged woman from some bygone era. And only a couple of times."

"Then I must caution you to be careful," he warned. "They never stay lovely for long."

End of excerpt.

If you enjoyed reading this
"Little Traveling Book"
please share it with someone!

If you have children (or know any), you may even enjoy browsing the *"mysteriously different books"* over at:

SummersIslandPress.com

www.ingramcontent.com/pod-product-compliance
Lightning Source LLC
Chambersburg PA
CBHW070448170726
48291CB00005B/1651